# Johnny and the Tool Chest

*Weekly Reader Children's Book Club presents*

# JOHNNY AND THE TOOL CHEST

*William D. Hayes*

PICTURES BY PAUL FRAME

ATHENEUM     NEW YORK

*To my mother*

Copyright © 1964 by William D. Hayes
All rights reserved
Library of Congress catalog card number 64-19560
Published simultaneously in Canada by
McClelland & Stewart Ltd.
Manufactured in the United States of America
Composition by Clarke & Way Inc., New York
Designed by David Rogers
Weekly Reader Children's Book Club Edition
Intermediate Division

# Contents

# A Beauty

"It sure is a beauty," Johnny Thornton said.

"It's a beauty, all right," Goober Wallace agreed. "But do you think your father will buy it for you? That's a lot of money."

"It isn't so much money," Johnny said. "Not when you realize that you get all this for it. My dad paid more than that for the power saw he bought for himself. And all he's made with it so far is a handle for a door on Mom's kitchen cabinet—and the door already had a handle. He won't let me go near that power saw; but even if he would, I'd still want my own set of tools. This set."

The two boys peered into the hardware store window. Johnny clicked his tongue. "The fact is," he said, "that's just about the most beautiful sight I ever saw." He allowed his eyes to move slowly over the contents of the window. He could almost feel the shiny tools in his hands. He imagined himself making some vast and towering structure, to the awe and admiration of all the town.

"I think I'll ask him after dinner," Johnny said. "That's when he reads the paper. He's usually in a pretty good mood then. I shouldn't have any trouble convincing him, though. It's such a bargain. That's the part I'll emphasize when I talk to him about it. It's such an obvious bargain."

"It may be obvious to you," Goober said. "But will it be obvious to your father?"

"It has to be," Johnny said. "I'll appeal to his intelligence."

"What are you going to build with it

4

first?" Goober asked.

"I haven't decided. Something big, though. Real big. Maybe a tree house. With a tool chest like that I could build just about anything I wanted to build—especially after all the experience I got in woodwork class last year. Nothing could stop me—not with a tool chest like this, and all that experience."

"Johnny, five pairs of book ends? That's *experience*?"

"And the footstool," Johnny said. "Don't forget the footstool."

"Well, I wasn't going to mention it," Goober said, "but I don't think you ever fixed it so it would sit quite level and not wobble around. At least I'm pretty sure you never got around to it."

"You obviously never heard of a rocking footstool," Johnny told him. "And anyway, I learned to plan how to build things. And that's almost more important than what to build."

"What will you use for materials?" Goober asked. "Wood costs money, too."

"I'll think about that later," Johnny said.

"Right now the important thing is to get that tool chest."

He fished a worn newspaper clipping from his shirt pocket. "It's a good thing I saw this ad in the paper this morning," he said. "Otherwise I might have missed the greatest bargain of the century." He compared the picture in the ad with the chest of tools, which rested, lone and regal, the sole occupant of the window.

"Come on," he said. "I want to get home before Dad gets there. I'm going to point out to him that I cleaned out the garage today. That should help put him in a good mood."

# The Approach

After dinner, Johnny sat on the sofa, folding and unfolding the advertisement. He hunched down almost to his shoulders and propped the clipping on his chest.

His father was in the big easy chair, reading the evening paper. His mother and younger sister Nancy were in the kitchen, where their voices mingled with the muffled clatter of dishes.

Johnny realized he would have only a few minutes alone with his father. But that should be plenty of time to bring up the tool chest. You had to approach these things in just the right way. If you brought up an important subject at the wrong time or in the wrong way, it was as bad as not bringing it up at all. Maybe worse.

*Thirty-nine dollars and ninety-five cents.* That was more money than Johnny had ever had at one time in his life.

He watched his father finish the editorial page and then turn to the funnies. Johnny could never understand what it was in grown-ups that made them put off the best things until last.

Mr. Thornton smiled at what he was reading.

Quickly Johnny went over in his mind the important facts about the tool chest. "Can't afford to slip up on anything," he told himself.

He decided to talk about the tools themselves and what a bargain they were, and not to mention the money at all. Not right away, that is.

8

Now his father was laughing out loud.

"Any second, now," Johnny thought.

But suddenly his father was folding the newspaper and starting to get up.

Panic swept over Johnny.

"POP, I NEED THIRTY-NINE DOL- LARS AND NINETY-FIVE CENTS," he blurted.

Mr. Thornton settled back in his chair. He folded his hands across his middle. He took a careful look at Johnny.

"Why do you need thirty-nine dollars and

ninety-five cents?" he asked.

Johnny held out the worn clipping.

"It's this tool chest," he said. "I guess it must be just about the best chest of tools that was ever on sale anywhere in the world—at such a saving, that is."

Mr. Thornton took the clipping.

"It's too good a bargain to pass up," Johnny said. "It would probably be a waste of money not to get it now, with all those tools it has. The price will never be this low again. The ad practically says so."

Mr. Thornton read the ad.

## PIONEER DAY SPECIAL

Our biggest offer of the summer

## THE DO-IT-YOURSELF TOOL CHEST

While they last— $39.95

Use our lay-away plan

A down payment will hold any article

HARDIN'S HARDWARE STORE

"It's a Pioneer Day special," Johnny said.

"I saw it in their window. The chest is painted red. It's about this long." He measured the distance with his hands.

"It does look like a pretty good buy, all right," Mr. Thornton said. "But are you sure you need all these tools?"

"Oh, I sure do. You bet," Johnny said.

"I see it has a hammer and saw," Mr. Thornton said. "We already have a hammer and saw."

"But I want a set of tools all my own. And besides, our saw is kind of rusty."

"And do you remember how it got rusty?" Mr. Thornton asked.

Johnny shuffled his feet. "I didn't know it was going to rain that day," he said. Then more cheerily he added, "This tool chest has a lot more things, too. It has a swell set of wood chisels and a mallet. And it has a vice and a brace and bit."

Mr. Thornton took out a pad and pencil. He began to write down some figures.

Johnny did not like the silence.

"Do you know what I found when I

cleaned out our garage today?" he said. "I found a big can of nails. They were under some old boxes. Those nails must be worth fifty cents, at least. Maybe more. With all those nails and that tool chest I could really build something important. Otherwise, we might be guilty of letting at least fifty cents worth of good nails go purely to waste."

Mr. Thornton went over the figures he had written. "I want to make sure this tool chest is really important to you," he said.

"Oh, it's important, all right. It's as important as everything," Johnny said.

"Well, then, here's what I'll do," Mr. Thornton said. "If you save up half the price of the tool chest, I'll put up the other half."

Johnny's stomach was a lump of ice.

"But that would take a long time," he wailed. "I'd have to get practically twenty dollars."

"I think an industrious boy could earn that much in a reasonable time," his father said. "That is, if it was important to him." He handed the clipping back to Johnny.

# *The Idea*

Mechanically Johnny stuffed the clipping into his pocket. He slumped farther into the sofa cushions and stared at nothing. A confusion of thoughts crowded his mind:

*That's the way with parents.*

*They don't understand the importance of time.*

*Right now is the time when things should happen.*

*Right now.*

*Not some time in the future.*

Johnny realized that his father was

speaking again.

"—but there is only one sure way to get money," Mr. Thornton was saying. "And that is to work for it. You know, very few people ever strike oil or find buried treasure."

"I guess they don't find buried treasure or things like that any more," Johnny said. "But some people sure get money without work. In contests, for instance. Contests aren't work. Remember last night on TV?—we saw somebody win a lot of money in a contest."

"Contest! Hey! That reminds me. Right there in the paper you were reading, Pop. There's going to be a Pioneer Day Contest."

Johnny took the paper and spread it out at his feet. "Sure. Two hundred and fifty dollars first prize for—here, it says right here —'for the front yard best decorated in the spirit of Pioneer Day.' I could build something in our yard that would win that contest. I know I could."

Johnny's eyes focused in the far distance.

"Oh boy. Two hundred and fifty dollars," he said. "With that much money, I can buy all the tools I want and some more besides."

"Now, look," Mr. Thornton said. "There will be a lot of people competing in that contest. And only one of them will win the prize money. If you want to decorate our yard for the contest, that's fine. You can have a lot of fun. But if you want to earn money for that tool chest, I think you had better work for it."

Johnny hunched down on the sofa and began to think hard.

"You've got a faraway look and a strange grin," Mr. Thornton said. "What are you thinking about?"

"I've got an idea for building something in our yard," Johnny said. "I know it would win the contest. But I need a lot more wood. Pop, do you suppose you could let me have

my allowance for a month ahead so I could buy the wood for—"

"Now, look here!" Mr. Thornton said. "No allowance money in advance, and that's final."

Johnny tried to look hurt.

Then Mr. Thornton said, "Some of the garages in the neighborhood must be cluttered up the way ours was before you cleaned it out. People would probably be glad to get rid of the old tires and scraps of wood and all the junk that piles up in their garages. If you set a fair price for your work, I think people would pay you to—"

"Scraps of wood!" Johnny almost shouted.

"What?" Mr. Thornton asked.

"You just gave me an idea, Pop. If there's a garage or basement or something in the neighborhood with a lot of old pieces of wood lying around in it, the people might give me the wood if I clean the place out."

Johnny's eyes grew bigger as he talked. "Then with all that wood I can build what I want to build for the contest. Then with the

16

two hundred and fifty dollars I win I can get that tool chest and a lot more wood. And then I can build anything I want to build. Nothing can stop me."

Mr. Thornton shook his head. "Why do they have to learn the hard way?" he said.

The kitchen noises stopped. Mrs. Thornton and Nancy came into the living room.

"What's Johnny got that funny look for?" Nancy asked.

"He has a get-rich-quick scheme," Mr. Thornton answered. "Other people have to *work* for money, but Johnny knows a better way to get it."

"I've got plans," Johnny said. "Big plans."

He started up the stairs. "I think I'd better do something about it now, or I might not even be able to sleep tonight."

"That will be the night," Mr. Thornton said.

From the closet in his room Johnny took a large sheet of brown laundry paper. He spread it on the floor and with a heavy black pencil began to print:

Plans for Pioneer Day Contest
BUFFALO BILL CHASING A BUFFALO

He drew in big, sweeping strokes.

He stepped back and looked at the draw-ing. Then he printed at the bottom of the paper:

TO BE LIFE SIZE

# *Search*

Johnny wakened early next morning.

He lay in bed and tried to picture the garages of the neighborhood. There were lots of things in them, he knew, but what about wood? He was not sure about that.

Except one.

He was sure about one. And that one was not a garage. It was a carriage house. On the ground floor of the carriage house was a pile of old lumber. There were long, straight pieces and short, narrow pieces. There were wide boards, and there were solid two-by-fours that would make good braces for just about anything.

"What I couldn't do with all that wood," Johnny said to himself.

He thought of the carriage house and the rest of the old-fashioned Spencer place at the end of the street. He had run errands a few times for Miss Spencer and had seen the lumber.

Why not try there? He could offer to clean out the carriage house if Miss Spencer would give him the wood. But the Spencer place had a spooky feeling. Johnny sometimes dreamed strange dreams about the huge house, with its tall towers and high, dark windows.

"I'll try the rest of the neighborhood first and see what I can find," he decided.

After breakfast Johnny did not even stop to make clear his opinions on minding one's own business.

"I heard all that paper rattling in your room last night," Nancy said. "What were you doing ?"

For an answer Johnny rolled his eyes upward and hurried out the front door.

There was only one good way to find out if garages had old pieces of wood stored in them. That was to look and see for himself. He could ask the owner, of course, but asking might lead to endless discussions about things that were not really important.

Out on the street the sun was bright. The day was going to be hot.

He squinted against the sunlight and tried to look into the garages as he passed. Deep shadows beyond the doorways was all that he could see.

At Goober Wallace's place Johnny went on by without trying to see into the garage.

This was because of *The Agreement.*

Johnny and Goober and the other boys in the neighborhood had long ago agreed not to ask each other's parents for odd jobs. Parents already had enough ideas about work to be done; there was no use suggesting more.

The Billingslys had a two-car garage and

only one car, he remembered. Plenty of extra room for a lot of stuff.

He stopped at the driveway and tried to peer into the garage. The doors were open toward the sun. A bright square of light on the floor was all he could see. He could make out nothing in the shadows beyond.

Then he remembered a story he had read about a detective who tracked down a criminal in the dark by looking into the darkness out of the edges of his eyes. The detective explained that the part of the eye away from the center is more sensitive to small amounts of light.

Johnny wondered if this would work in the daytime. He decided to try it.

He turned, a little at a time, and peered sideways into the shadows.

He could not see what was in the garage.

He turned around the other way and tried it again. He turned, a little at a time, until the garage almost disappeared from sight. He realized that his eyes were bulging and his mouth was stretched to one side.

22

Then he realized something else.

Someone was on the porch. It was Mr. Billingsly. Mr. Billingsly stood with his arms folded. He was watching Johnny very carefully.

Johnny hurried on down the street and around the corner.

"There's always Miss Spencer's carriage house," he said to himself. "But I'm not that desperate yet."

From the front of the long driveway at

the Weldons, Johnny could dimly make out forms in the garage. But he could not see what they were.

"Maybe if I could get the light just right," he said to himself. He shaded his eyes and moved to one side.

"Johnny Thornton! Are you standing in my flower bed?" Mrs. Weldon shrieked.

Johnny looked down and saw that one foot was in the soft earth among the sweet peas.

"I'm sorry, Mrs. Weldon. I'm awful sorry," he said. He stooped and hastily smoothed the earth over the footprint. Then he hurried on.

The Birdlows had recently built a dog house. "How much wood can you have left over from a dog house?" Johnny wondered.

"No harm in finding out," he told himself.

The big double garage was open, but it was far back from the street. Johnny took a few steps into the driveway.

Then things happened fast.

There was a growling sound. Something furry and brown cleared a back yard fence and landed running toward Johnny.

In one bound Johnny was at the birch by the front sidewalk. He grasped a limb and swung into the tree.

The big dog leaped and growled.

Johnny looked down, thinking. It was a big dog. There might be quite a lot of wood left.

A door slammed.

"Prince! Prince!" Mrs. Birdlow shouted. She ran to the dog and seized his collar.

"Johnny!" she exclaimed. "I'm terribly

sorry. Why, Prince went over that fence as if it weren't even there. We'll have to do something about that."

Johnny jumped down from the tree.

"I can't understand it," Mrs. Birdlow said. "He usually doesn't make any fuss unless someone comes in the yard."

"Well, I guess maybe I did go a little way into the driveway," Johnny said. "I was trying to see if—uh—Mrs. Birdlow, do you have any wood?"

"Wood?"

"Yes, ma'am. Old pieces of wood. I need quite a lot of them, in fact. I thought maybe if you had some you didn't need, I could— well, I would be very happy to work for it."

"Well, let me see," she said. "There were a few pieces left over from building the house for Prince. They're back by the garage. You're welcome to them if you want them."

When Johnny looked at the little pile of scrap lumber against the fence he said, "Well, thanks, Mrs. Birdlow. I guess they aren't quite big enough. Thanks, anyway, Mrs.

Birdlow."

Johnny walked back with his hands in his pockets thinking. He walked on past his own house. Nancy was standing on the porch. "Where are you going, Johnny?" she called after him.

"I don't know," he said. "I'm not real sure. But I'll think of something."

# *A Bargain*

The old Spencer house at the end of the street grew bigger as Johnny came nearer. He paused at the sagging iron gate. Back beyond the winding driveway, the huge main house and the carriage house lay almost hidden in the shade of the trees.

"I wonder if I can make a deal with Miss Spencer for that wood?" Johnny asked himself. He decided to think about it a little more. He strolled along the rutted sidewalk, plowed by ancient tree roots. "No use rushing into

28

anything," he said to himself.

He leaned against the rusty iron fence and hooked his thumbs in his pockets. Now and then he took a look at the old place through the fence. He remembered the re-marks people sometimes made about Miss Spencer. "Living all alone like that in that big, old house," they said. Or, "Never going anywhere and never spending any money." But more often they made the vague accusa-tion that she was "peculiar."

"Who needs lumber?" he muttered. Then after a moment he shrugged and said, "I do."

As he walked up the long driveway, he saw Miss Spencer standing on a wooden crate at the side of the house. She dipped a brush in a large bucket of paint beside her and dabbed at a window sill.

"Hello, Johnny," she said, without looking away from her work.

"Hello, Miss Spencer," Johnny said.

He saw the sprawling pile of boards in the carriage house.

"Miss Spencer," he said, "I'll clean out the carriage house for you if you will let me have all those pieces of wood that are piled in there."

"Hmmmm," Miss Spencer said.

Johnny waited.

Miss Spencer made a few dabs with the brush and then said, "That lumber is worth a good bit. Some of it is the oak flooring left from repairs in the dining room."

Then after a few moments she said, "That carriage house certainly needs cleaning,

30

though. If you will help me finish painting these window sills and then help me clean out the carriage house, too, I'll let you have the lumber."

Johnny said, "That's fair enough, Miss Spencer. But I'd like to get it all done as soon as possible. I'm going to build something important with that wood—something big. It's for the Pioneer Day Contest. The contest ends Friday night. I guess there isn't much time."

"We will take enough time to get the work done right," Miss Spencer said. "First there are the sills on this side of the house to finish, and then there are those on the other side."

She indicated a bucket by the corner of the porch. "You'll find another paint brush there. You take those low sills where you can stand on the ground."

Johnny liked the smell of paint. There was pleasure in drawing the wet brush across the wood.

From time to time he glanced at the carriage house.

"Better be careful and watch what you're doing," Miss Spencer said.

"Yes, ma'am," Johnny said. But he soon found that when he bent over to dip the brush in the bucket, he could look back and see into the carriage house. There was no harm in this, that he could see, and it would help him figure out the best way to start building the buffalo.

The plans took shape as he painted. "Those long pieces leaning against the wall there," he thought, "they ought to make a good framework for Buffalo Bill's horse and probably even part of—"

"LOOK OUT!" Miss Spencer screamed.

It was too late.

Johnny had caught the edge of the paint bucket with his brush. He grasped the bucket and set it upright. But not before white paint flooded the ground and flowed through the grass.

"I'm sorry, Miss Spencer."

"I told you to watch what you were doing, Johnny. That's more than a half-gallon of good paint gone to waste. And look at my poor grass.

"Carelessness!

"Just carelessness!"

Miss Spencer put her hands on her hips. "Now how are you going to pay for that paint?" she asked.

"I—I don't know, Miss Spencer. I haven't got any money. Except maybe about seven cents."

"Well," she said, "it isn't so much the money, but there's an important principle involved."

"There is?"

"Yes, there is. I think you should pay for

your carelessness, and for the damage you did. You don't have to pay in money, but there are other ways. I could use your help, Johnny. There are things I have to do to get ready for Pioneer Day. There will be errands to run."

Johnny felt a strange sensation in his stomach. He saw precious time slipping away. When was he going to build Buffalo Bill?

"So, if you will run errands for me, say, a half-hour a day for the next three days," Miss Spencer said, "I will consider the paint paid for."

Johnny squirmed.

"I've got an awful lot to do," he said.

"I think you should be responsible for that paint, Johnny."

"Yes, ma'am." He bit his lip and thought. "All right, Miss Spencer. I'll run the errands."

"And just to keep it on a businesslike basis," she said, "I think we should make it at the same time every day. Will three-thirty be all right?"

"Yes, ma'am. Three-thirty will be all right."

# *Lumber*

They finished the window sills a little before noon.

At lunch Johnny announced casually to
his mother and Nancy, "I made a deal for
some lumber."

"That's good," his mother said. "Did you
make a fair exchange all the way around?"

"Oh, sure," Johnny said. "Sure, I guess
so. If everything goes all right this afternoon,
that is."

He did not mention the spilled paint.

After lunch he took out the plans he had drawn on the laundry paper. Those long pieces of lumber in the carriage house had given him more ideas.

"No use doing things in a puny way," he said as he re-drew parts of the plans with a soft red pencil. "Buffalo Bill deserves the best —the best and the biggest."

Before going back to Miss Spencer's, Johnny rode his bike the few blocks to Hardin's hardware store. He stood leaning on the handlebars, one foot resting on the pedal. He looked at the tools separately, and he knew what he would do with each one.

"So long, until I win that contest," he said as he rode away.

Miss Spencer was already in the carriage house. She propped her chin on one hand and looked about.

There was a mustiness in the old place that made Johnny want to shiver. But at the same time he was eager to see what was there, to hold the pieces of wood in his hands.

The cracked leather of an old harness

36

hung on its wall peg. There was an elaborate
vase almost as tall as Johnny. There were
trunks with rounded tops, huge books in
crumbling leather bindings, old magazines,
and a stack of dusty china plates.

"You might as well start by carrying out
the lumber," Miss Spencer said. "Then we
will see what's what."

Johnny built and rebuilt the horse and
buffalo in his mind as he dragged the long
pieces into the yard.

Then the two of them worked together, moving, stacking, sorting. Johnny lifted and pushed and carried. It was a hot, dusty after-noon.

At last Johnny finished sweeping the rough boards of the first floor. He leaned on the broom and mopped the sweat from his face.

"What about the upstairs?" he asked.

"The upstairs?" Miss Spencer repeated. She looked toward the upper floor as if she had not known it was there. "That was Grandfather's studio. I haven't been up there since—" She did not finish.

"Let's have a look at it," she said.

The door squeaked and groaned as they stepped into the room. A dull orange light poured through the windows.

Huge picture frames leaned against the walls. An easel still held its canvas. Several long brushes lay at its base. A palette rested on a high stool, its paint cracked and dried in the dust.

Johnny tiptoed closer. There on the

canvas in bold strokes was the beautiful face of a young girl.

Johnny looked closer at the painting. Then suddenly he looked at Miss Spencer's face.

"Holy smoke!" he said under his breath. "Holy smoke!"

"I think we will leave everything just as it is," Miss Spencer said.

When they were in the yard she said, "You're a good worker, Johnny. Thanks for your help. I'm glad to get this place straightened up. And the lumber is yours."

Johnny sized up the precious pile. It looked big—and heavy. He'd have to carry it all home today if he was going to begin his project tomorrow morning. He mopped his face again. Maybe he could get it all home before dark—if they would only let him hurry through supper. That was a problem he worked on from time to time: How to hurry through a meal without appearing to hurry at all.

As Johnny picked up the first pieces of

lumber, Miss Spencer said, "Until tomorrow, then. Three-thirty."

*The errands! The spilled paint!* He had almost forgotten.

"Yes, ma'am. Tomorrow at three-thirty," he said.

He started down the driveway, dragging the two longest boards. "She's pretty strict," he said to himself. "But she's all right. I think I like her." He looked back at the house and carriage house. "And as for the old place itself, I'm not sure I like it, but I'll bet I won't let it give me the creeps again."

The wood was solid and heavy. He soon found that he could manage only a few pieces at a time. The two blocks between his house and the Spencer place seemed longer with each trip. As he carried the lumber, he tried to imagine how the huge figures would look when they were finished, and what he would feel like when he was the winner of an important contest.

"It's going to be fun," he said to himself. "And it sure beats working."

40

# The Start

At breakfast next morning Johnny held the half-folded plans in his lap. He studied them from time to time.

"What have you got there?" Nancy asked. "What's that big piece of paper for?"

"Plans."

"What kind of plans?"

"Plans for the Pioneer Day Contest. I'm going to build something big."

"Let me help you build it."

Johnny looked at the plans. The words LIFE SIZE stood out from the paper. For life size, he would need help. The project was taking on new proportions. In his imagination he saw himself as the overseer of a vast building project, with a crew of workmen carrying out his orders.

"This is man's work," he said to Nancy. "How are you at handling carpenter's tools?"

"Oh, I'd be real good at it. I know I would."

"Come on, Nancy," he said. "I'll give you a try."

As they started out the door, Mrs. Thornton said, "What is this Pioneer Day project going to do to my front yard?"

"It's only for a few days," Johnny said. "It's worth it for fame and fortune. And two hundred and fifty dollars."

First he nailed a square of cardboard to a stake. With a soft black pencil he lettered the words:

THINK BIG

Then he drove the stake with the cardboard into the ground.

He spread the plans on the grass and

weighted them with blocks of wood.

"We'll put Buffalo Bill and the horse on this side of the walk, and the buffalo over there," he said. "They're going to be life size. Maybe bigger."

While he prepared to go over the plans once more, making final changes, he handed the hammer to Nancy. "Hammer on this," he said, pointing to a long two-by-four.

"What for?" Nancy asked.

"You'll see," he told her. "Just hammer away."

She held the hammer with both hands

and hit the piece of wood.

"You'll do better with one hand," Johnny said. "Make it good and loud."

He measured long boards and checked his plans while Nancy hammered.

"What good is this doing?" she asked. She was panting.

"Just keep it up," Johnny said. "Make it loud."

He went on measuring.

Nancy went on hammering.

Goober Wallace was the first to arrive.

"Hey! What's all the hammering? What are you making?" Goober wanted to know.

"Something big," Johnny answered. Then with intense concentration, he grasped the crosscut saw and began to cut along a black line. "It's for the Pioneer Day contest."

"Oh boy! Is it a tree house?" Goober asked.

"What?" Johnny asked, looking up from his sawing.

"A tree house," Goober said. "We were going to make a tree house, weren't we?"

44

"Oh, *that*," Johnny said. "That was just an idea. I've gone way beyond that. What I'm making is for the big contest."

"Wow!" Goober said. "Can I help?"

"Have you got a hammer and saw?" Johnny asked.

"There's a hammer at the house," Goober said. "I guess we haven't got a saw right now."

Johnny sawed away thoughtfully. "Okay. Get the hammer."

Goober was gone on the run.

Soon Al Ketcham rode up on his bicycle. "What's all the hammering and sawing?" he asked.

"It's a kind of a secret," Johnny said. "But it's something big. It's for Pioneer Day. I'm making it for the contest."

"Can I help? I can build things pretty good. You don't have to pay me anything if you win the contest."

"Have you got a hammer and saw?"

"I think so. If I can find them."

"Find them. I can sure use your help, all right."

Al rode away.

"Shall I go on hammering?" Nancy asked.

"You bet. Only now I want you to hammer nails. Drive one about halfway through here, and one here and here." He marked $X$'s on the long timber.

Within an hour there were four volunteers, three hammers, a coping saw, a brace and bit, and a dried-up paint brush. Nancy had been promoted to the coping saw and was cutting out a rifle for Buffalo Bill.

"Good work, boys," Johnny said.

Much of the time Johnny was on his hands and knees over the plans. He made changes with a red pencil as the building went along.

"Is this where this leg goes?" Goober asked, holding a length of two-by-four to the frame.

"Absolutely," Johnny said. "Nail it on." He consulted the plans, and saw that they called for the leg to be placed farther back. But the final *wham, wham, wham* of the hammer told him that Goober had already carried out orders. Johnny shrugged. He marked the leg from the plans with a big *X*, and drew the leg in its new location.

By noon the yard was an array of scattered lumber and partly built framework.

"Oh boy!" someone yelled.

Mrs. Thornton had appeared on the porch with a tray of sandwiches and a tall, tinkling pitcher.

"All of you deserve some lunch," she said. "Come on over in the shade. I phoned your mothers. It's all right with them if you have a kind of picnic lunch with us. Who likes ham? These are chicken on this side." She was pouring the lemonade.

The boys shuffled around, grinning. Nancy went straight for the tray and grasped a ham sandwich in both hands.

The boys took places on the steps and along the edge of the porch to eat.

When they were back at work, Johnny said, "I guess we're about ready to stand up the main part of the framework. Then we can see how the rest of it will fit."

Gradually a crowd of onlookers gathered at the curb and on the sidewalk. Bicycles were parked, and some served as props for their owners.

There was something different about these newcomers. Johnny sensed the difference before he saw it.

"Maybe some of them would like to help," Goober suggested.

Johnny looked at the group at the curb. He shook his head. "I don't think so." he said. "They're strictly sidewalk supervisors. They just want to look."

The boys at the curb commented from time to time on the progress of the work. One of them looked in mock horror at the structures going up on the lawn. "What are they going to be?" he asked. "Another pair of book ends?"

There was laughter from the curb.

"My brother says he thinks one of them is going to be a buffalo," the boy said. "I guess he doesn't know much about buffaloes."

More laughter.

"Could you nail the buffalo's head on again?" another boy called, much louder than the first. "Lefty didn't get here in time for that—that is, if it *is* a head."

"You mean if it's a buffalo," the first boy said, and followed the remark with a hoot of laughter.

Goober threw down his saw and started toward the curb. Johnny put a hand on Goober's arm. "Skip it," Johnny said. "Let them talk all they want to. Who cares?"

Goober stood for a long moment, looking at the group of boys. Then he turned and went back to his sawing.

"Sorry Lefty missed the nailing of the head," Johnny said. "No time for a repeat. Only one show today."

There was a ripple of laughter. Several of the bigger, louder boys rode away, leaving a hard core of genuinely awe-struck bystanders to carry on the important work of watching.

Slowly the framework was rounded out

50

to give the animals thick, life-size bodies.

Something in the back of Johnny's mind was nagging him. He tried to push it away. But the feeling was still there.

Then he remembered.

*Errands !*

*Miss Spencer !*

He ran to the door and looked at the clock. 3:45.

He jumped on his bicycle.

"I'll be back pretty soon," he said. "In about a half-hour."

He felt them watching him as he rode to the Spencer house.

When Miss Spencer opened the door, Johnny said, "I guess I'm a little late."

"Yes, you are a little late. But it's all right."

She gave him a slip of paper. "Here is a list of groceries I want you to get for me at Johnson's. Then if there is time, I want you to run this dress over to Mrs. Finley on Baker Street. She is going to hem it for me."

Johnson's store was not crowded. Johnny was back in less than twenty minutes.

51

"This is a lace dress," Miss Spencer told him. "Please be careful with it."

Johnny studied the white lace.

"Do you have a bag for it?" he asked.

"I don't want it crumpled in a bag," she said. "I'm afraid you'll have to carry it like this. It's only four short blocks. Maybe you had better walk. You might have difficulty with it on your bicycle."

"Oh, I carry everything on my bicycle," Johnny said. He looked at the dress again. "Just about everything."

To get to Mrs. Finley's the alleys would be safer than the streets, he decided. There would not be so many people in the alleys— people to wonder about a lace dress.

Mrs. Finley swept the dress from his arm and thanked him in a flood of words. She was grateful to have the work, she said, and was thankful to Johnny for bringing the dress, and what would she do without the good people of the world, and wasn't the weather hot?

The hardware store was only two blocks away.

"Better not take the time," Johnny told himself. But when he saw that the bicycle seemed to be heading itself in that direction, with almost no help from him, he added, "It'll only take a minute." He stopped long enough to read the sign in the window. The afternoon sun beat down on the bright red tool chest.

As he rode along the streets he saw other projects being built for the contest.

One of them looked as if it was going to be a huge map of the United States, with the

city a shining star outshining all other cities.

Several people were working on a display showing a tall figure in flowing robes holding high the torch of culture and achievement.

In the next block was a display showing a smiling pioneer sitting on top of the world.

"Corn," Johnny thought. "Real corn. Wait till the contest judges see my Buffalo Bill."

There was a different sound in Johnny's yard as he rode up. The hammering and sawing had stopped, and there were loud voices.

"Here's Johnny, now," Goober Wallace shouted. "Just ask him."

Al Ketcham was about to saw the buffalo's tail short, but Goober was holding back Al's sawing hand with his own.

"I know how long a buffalo's tail is," Al said. "Let go my hand."

"I saw a buffalo once," Goober said. "And its tail was a lot longer than that."

"I tell you what," Johnny said. "I'll fix the buffalo's tail. Why don't you fellows saw up some pieces to brace the frame along here.

54

We'll need enough to go along both sides."

The hammering and sawing went on until late afternoon.

"I guess I'll have to go," Goober was the first to announce. Johnny knew the others would be leaving soon.

He stood back and looked at the results of the day's work. "It's beginning to look like something," he said. "But there's still a long way to go. Maybe by tomorrow or day after tomorrow it will begin to look like Buffalo Bill on a horse chasing a buffalo."

# *Progress*

By noon the next day there were the same number of volunteers as the day before. But except for Goober and Al, they were all new hands. This made the work go slowly.

Johnny explained the procedure to each recruit. He wondered if he might save time by doing the nailing and sawing himself, instead of explaining it to the newcomers.

There was a knot in his stomach as he stepped back and studied the structures. They didn't look any nearer finished than they had three hours before, he had to admit.

Mr. Billingsly strolled by and asked, "How is it going, Johnny?"

"Well, sir," Johnny said, "the time is going fast, but the building is pretty slow."

As before, there was the audience at the curb and on the sidewalk.

Early in the afternoon an ice cream wagon stopped. "Hey, get your ice cream here. Free floor show," the man called. "Right this way. Get your ice cream." He did a good business for nearly a half-hour.

A car with PRESS on a windshield card went by slowly several times.

"Maybe besides winning the contest, I'll get my picture in the paper, too," Johnny said to himself. He daydreamed on this pleasant prospect. The hammer he wielded came to a halt in mid-air. But the knot in his stomach reminded him that time was short, and he swung the hammer harder than ever.

Later, as he rode toward Miss Spencer's, he thought, "Maybe I should have made them smaller. They won't be any good if we can't finish them by tomorrow night in time for the contest, no matter how big they are."

When Miss Spencer came to the door, she said, "I'll be easy on you today, Johnny. If you will return these books to the library for me, I'll let you get back to your work. How is it coming along?"

"Well, not too bad, I guess. But there sure is a lot more to do."

He thought she might tell him to skip the errands for the next day. But instead she said, "I'll have something important for you to do tomorrow at three-thirty."

"I'll be here," he said. He rode away balancing the books on his head and steadying them with one hand.

There was the hush of a midsummer afternoon about the library. From somewhere came the drone of an electric fan. Johnny left Miss Spencer's books at the desk. He wished there was time to look for a book for himself.

"Better get moving," he thought.

Several of the contest entries along the way were almost finished.

"Corn. Real corn," Johnny muttered.

A quick ride by the hardware store, a glance at the tool chest, and he headed for home.

From a block away he could see that the horse and the buffalo both were far from finished. There were many gaps in the framework.

There were still gaps to fill when the volunteers began to drift away at the end of the afternoon.

"Only one more day," Johnny said when he and Nancy were left alone in the yard.

# *Pressure*

Only the hum of a milk delivery truck broke the stillness of early morning when Johnny woke.

"Too early to start sawing and hammering," he thought. "But not too early to measure and mark."

When he reached the front yard, no one was on the street.

Several blocks away there were other partly completed contest entries. Their brilliant colors glistened gaudily in the early morning sun. No one was at work on the other projects yet.

"The early bird wins the contest," Johnny thought as he set to work.

He measured and marked pieces for the sides of the buffalo. Then he selected a long board and laid it flat on the ground. He went to the garage and took a small can of black paint from its hiding place above a rafter.

In large block letters along the length of the board he printed:

BUFFALO BILL—
OUR GREATEST HERO

Under this he printed:

ENTERED IN PIONEER DAY CONTEST
BY JOHNNY THORNTON

Then after thinking for several moments he added:

(with help from a lot of other persons)

With short sticks he propped the board at a slant facing the street.

Now from the neighborhood there came familiar morning noises—the slamming of a door and the rush of a car engine starting. Soon the sounds from his own house and a gentle wafting from the kitchen told him there would probably be pancakes for breakfast.

He went inside to investigate.

"You had me worried," Mr. Thornton said with a grin. "I thought you were going to miss a meal for the first time in your life."

"Yeah, sure," Johnny said as he buttered a stack of pancakes.

And when he had eaten his usual amount he said, "I guess I'd better have a couple more, Mom. It's going to be a big day. I have to store up a lot of energy."

"I had counted on that," she said. "I made some extra."

"Are all those boys coming to help you today?" Nancy asked.

"Sure. I guess so. Most of them, anyway. They're good guys. You can depend on them."

"Can I help, too?"

"Okay. Sure. There are several things you can do. A lot of the pieces are measured off. I did that this morning. You can saw if you want to. You'll have to be pretty careful."

After they had worked for a while, Johnny said, "I wonder where everybody is."

The sun was climbing high.

Al rode by late in the morning to say he had to mow the lawn. He wouldn't be able to help.

"That's okay," Johnny said. "Thanks anyway. You did swell yesterday and the day before."

Goober was the only member of the crew who came to work. He wouldn't be able to stay very long, he explained. Relatives were coming for the Pioneer Day weekend. He had to help at home.

63

"Every little bit helps," Johnny said. "It's going pretty well, I guess. There's still a lot to do, though."

After Goober left, Johnny studied the buffalo. The unfinished sides gaped at him. His muscles tightened as he looked over the plans and tried to figure out shortcuts. His breathing was rapid. The time pressed in on him. He could not remember ever before being irritated by the heat, but now the sweat smarted in his eyes, and he slapped at the beads that stood out on his face.

After lunch, Johnny felt sure there would be no more help from outside.

He whistled a fast tune as he worked. The tune and the hammering and sawing went faster as the time for errands came closer.

When he knew there was only a little time left, he pounded each nail harder and faster.

"I could run errands for Miss Spencer some other time," he said. He emphasized the words with hard hammer blows. Sweat dripped from his face.

"A half-hour now would wreck everything," he said. "The contest starts tonight. That sure isn't much time. It will take every bit of that to fix these things up the way I want them. I can run errands for Miss Spencer some other time. Maybe even tonight after we finish these."

"Did you promise her?" Nancy asked.

# Delays

Johnny threw down the hammer. He kicked at a block of wood and sent it spinning across the yard.

He got on his bicycle and rode away.

"If you will pick up the dress, I won't need you for anything else today," Miss Spencer told him. "It should take you just a few minutes. Mrs. Finley promised the dress for three-thirty. The rest of the time is your own. I know you are still working on the contest."

"Thanks, Miss Spencer," he said.

When Mrs. Finley came to the door, she was holding a small crying child in one arm and a bottle of milk in the other.

"Johnny Thornton! Goodness sakes!" she exclaimed. "Is it three-thirty already? I tried to call Miss Spencer back, but my phone is out of order. Now, you just sit right here and wait. I hope you'll excuse the mess. I'll have the dress ready in a while."

Mrs. Finley set the crying child down in a playpen. "Little Beemis has been fretting all afternoon," she said. "Must be the heat. It's about to get me, too."

She went to the sewing table. "Everything happens at once," she said above the crying of little Beemis. "My boy Orville is over at the Willoughbys. I need him here real bad. But I can't call them because my phone won't work, and I can't call the phone company for the same reason. Everything happens at once."

"It sure does," Johnny said to himself.

Beemis' crying subsided to a singsong rhythm. He studied Johnny intently.

"Once upon a time there were three bears," Johnny said.

Beemis began to laugh.

"I didn't know I was that good," Johnny said. "But here goes." He got down on all fours.

"A great big papa bear." Johnny pushed up as high as he could on the tips of his fingers and toes.

"And a middle-sized mama bear." He put his knees and elbows on the floor.

68

"And a wee little baby bear." He brought his elbows and knees together and shrunk as small as he could.

Beemis laughed and jumped up and down.

Johnny looked up from the floor. "Mrs. Finley, how long will it take to get the dress ready?"

"Oh, it won't take long. Let me see. Maybe twenty or twenty-five minutes."

"Twenty or twenty-five minutes?" Johnny repeated. "Couldn't I just take it to Miss Spencer the way it is?"

"Oh, goodness, no," Mrs. Finley said. "I couldn't let you do that. You just wait, and I'll have it in a jiffy."

"I've already lived up to my part of the bargain," Johnny thought. "It isn't my fault if other people don't do the same."

There was a stillness in the air that was stifling. He wanted to run from the house and jump on his bicycle and ride away.

Beemis began to fret again.

"One morning the three bears went out

into the forest to pick berries." Johnny crooked his arm like the top of a basket and picked imaginary berries with the other hand.

Beemis stopped fretting.

"I wish my boy Orville would come home," Mrs. Finley said. "I've got things for him to do. I wish the phone company would fix my phone. But they can't fix it if they don't know it needs fixing, I suppose."

She sat sewing and shaking her head.

"While the bears were away, a little girl named Goldilocks went into their house."

Beemis listened, wide-eyed.

Johnny watched while Mrs. Finley made unsuccessful passes at threading a needle. He fidgeted with sympathetic muscular action and made imaginary thrusts at the needle himself.

Beads of sweat stood out on him in the tension and stifling heat of the little frame house. "Maybe if I could just go out and stretch my legs a little," he said to himself. He jumped up.

"Mrs. Finley," he said, "there's a telephone office not too far from here. I'll go tell them about your telephone."

"Oh, I don't know what I would do without the good people of—" But Johnny was out the door before she could finish.

Beemis started to whimper.

Johnny stuck his head back in the door. "Goldilocks ate the little bear's breakfast. When the bears came home, they found Goldilocks asleep in the little bear's bed. Goldilocks woke up and ran away. That's the jist of the story. Other things happen, but they don't matter much."

The only sound that Johnny heard as he rode away was the loud crying of little Beemis.

"I wonder if I'm spreading myself too thin," Johnny said.

At the telephone office, the lady told him they would send someone to fix Mrs. Finley's phone.

"I might as well go the few blocks farther on to the Willoughbys and tell Orville his mother wants him," he decided. "A few more minutes can't make much difference now."

In a vacant lot near the Willoughbys, some boys were playing softball.

"Your mother wants you at home," Johnny called to Orville.

Orville had just stepped up to the plate. He wielded the bat impatiently. He squared off and waited for the pitch.

"Right now," Johnny said.

Orville waited a long moment. Then he dropped the bat. He yanked his own bicycle from a tangle of bicycles at the corner of the lot.

The two boys rode back together.

Mrs. Finley met them at the door. "Bless me, you're just in time," she said to Johnny. Then she looked squarely at Orville. Orville looked at the floor.

Mrs. Finley clipped a few threads and placed the dress over Johnny's arm. "Hold it just like that and it will be all right," she said.

With the lace dress fluttering over his arm, Johnny started riding toward the hardware store. "If I ride fast enough, maybe nobody will see me," he told himself.

Just a glimpse of the tool chest would be enough. He turned out of the alley and raced by the store. A flashing reflection of light on the window was all he could see.

"Must have gone *too* fast," he told himself. He turned around. He stopped at the curb and stared at the window.

The tool chest was gone.

He held the dress awkwardly and tried to decide what to do. Then holding his head high and carrying the dress like a flag, he went into the store.

"Excuse me," he said to the clerk. "The tool chest. The one that was in the window—have you still got it on special?"

"I think we sold the last one today," the clerk said. "Just a minute."

He called toward the back of the store. "Did we sell the last one of those tool chests?"

"That's right," came the answer. "Somebody made a down payment on it today. Lay-away plan. We're holding it."

"Thanks," Johnny said mechanically.

As he rode along, hardly seeing the street, he thought, "There must be other tool chests." But he could not force back the tight feeling in his throat.

At the Spencer driveway, he stopped and looked down the street toward his own house.

Who were all those people?

A crowd had gathered in his yard and on the sidewalk. A man was holding something that looked like a big camera. A car with a card on the windshield was at the curb.

Johnny started pedaling toward his house. Then he remembered the dress. Quickly he wheeled and raced up the driveway. He skidded to a stop and jumped to the porch. Miss Spencer was at the door.

"Johnny, I want to thank you over and over again," she said. She took the dress. "Mrs. Finley called. They fixed her telephone. She told me all about the nice things you did."

"That's all right, Miss Spencer. You're welcome," he said. "I've got to go, now."

He jumped on the bicycle and pedaled down the driveway.

# Finished

He saw the car pull away from his house. As the car came closer Johnny could see the word PRESS on the windshield. A man sitting by the driver was writing in a big pad of paper.

The crowd was still in the yard. Nancy was sitting on top of the buffalo, waving and laughing.

"Nancy's picture is going to be in the paper," one of the boys shouted as Johnny rode up.

"Picture? Nancy's picture? How come?"

76

"They took pictures of her sitting on the buffalo," Al said.

"They wanted to talk to you, Johnny," Nancy said. "They couldn't wait any longer. It's for tomorrow's paper. Your name will be in it, too. I told them all about you, Johnny— how it was all your idea and everything."

The tightness tugged at Johnny's throat. There was a burning in his eyes.

"Can we help you finish building them?" Opie Warren asked.

"Yeah. Sure," Johnny managed to say.

He went into the house.

He went to his room and shut the door. He stretched out face down on the bed.

He did not try to hold back any longer. But the muffled sounds in the pillow were lost in the sounds of hammering and sawing and laughing and shouting from the front yard.

By the time Johnny appeared in the yard again, the hammering and sawing had stopped.

"How do you like them?" Opie asked. "Not bad, huh?"

"They look swell, guys," Johnny said. "They look real swell."

He walked around the huge figures. "I guess there isn't much left to do except paint on the faces," he said.

Johnny held the can of paint like an artist's palette. With steady hand, he painted the eyes and mouth, first on the buffalo, then on the horse.

"How are you going to reach Buffalo Bill's face?" someone asked. "Bert Buford took his stepladder home."

Everybody laughed.

Johnny set the paint down. He thought a moment. Then he slapped his hands together.

"Okay, everybody into the act," he shouted. "Let's make a pyramid."

"Yea!"

"Hooray!"

"Let's go!"

"Hey!"

The shouts mingled with a general scramble. Nancy backed away.

"Okay. First we need four strong backs,"

Johnny shouted. "Come on. No experience necessary."

Luther Jarvis shuffled forward, grinning. Johnny picked out three more of the bigger boys. "Come on, you, you, and you," he said. "Let's go."

In seconds the four boys were on their hands and knees, forming the first layer of the pyramid. "Out of my way!" Al Ketcham shouted. He made a great show of running as if to jump with all fours on top of the first layer. Then, amid yells from the four, he carefully climbed up, and others climbed up beside him, and still others on top of them. Last of all, Johnny made his way to the top of the weaving, yelling heap.

"Okay, Nancy. Let's have that can of paint."

Nancy gave the paint to a boy on the second layer.

"Easy does it," Johnny said as the paint was handed up one layer at a time. "Okay. Steady, men." He painted on Buffalo Bill's eyes and mouth. Then with quick strokes he

gave the hero a tuft of flying hair.

"That does it," he said. He started the can of paint down. When it was handed to Nancy, the pyramid collapsed in a scramble of tumbling and laughing and shouting.

Johnny stood back and admired the finished work. Buffalo Bill grinned down foolishly at him.

That evening Johnny said to his father, "Dad, a lot of guys helped me build those things for the contest. Nancy, too. If I win the contest, I guess I ought to divide up some of the prize money with them."

"I'm glad to hear you say that, Son," his father said. "I think you're right in feeling that way."

"As for the tool chest, that's out," Johnny said. "They sold the last one today. They told me so at the store."

"The tool chest?" Mr. Thornton said. "I made a down payment on that tool chest. I asked them to call me if they got down to the last one."

Johnny sat up straight. "Oh boy!"

"They'll hold it for ninety days," Mr. Thornton said. "So even if you don't win the contest, you still ought to have plenty of time to earn your half of the money."

"Oh boy!" Johnny said. "Now I've *got* to win that prize money."

"Well, tomorrow's the day," Mr. Thornton said. "We'll know in the morning. Winners will be announced in the morning paper."

# The Announcement

When Johnny woke next morning, he could hear voices in the street. He went to the window.

Several people were on the sidewalk looking at Buffalo Bill. Johnny tried to pick something from their words that would tell him if he had won the contest. One of the men wore a cowboy hat and a bandana. A car slowed down as it went by.

Johnny had the feeling that more should be happening. This was the day. This was

Pioneer Day. Someone should be pounding on his door and telling him he had won first prize.

Almost immediately there came a knock at his door.

"Breakfast," his mother said.

At the head of the stairs Johnny stopped to listen.

"There she is. Just as big as life," Mrs. Thornton was saying. "Nancy, you're famous."

Johnny took the stairs two at a time. When he ran into the dining room, the morning paper was spread on the table.

Johnny looked over Nancy's shoulder. On a page of photos was a picture of Nancy on the buffalo.

"Your buffalo shows up real well," Mrs. Thornton said. "And right under the picture it tells how it was all your idea."

"Who won the contest?" Johnny asked.

Mr. Thornton turned to the front page.

PIONEER DAY
CONTEST WINNERS CHOSEN

Across three columns were photographs of the winners, first, second and third places. Johnny did not recognize any of them.

"Your name is here, too, Johnny," Mr. Thornton said, pointing. There, in the middle of a long, gray column, Johnny read:

JOHNNY THORNTON, 831 EAST FILMORE STREET.

The column was headed:

*Honorable Mention*

Johnny sat down at the table and stared at his plate.

When his mother brought in the breakfast, he ate without noticing what he was eating.

After breakfast he slumped onto the couch in the living room.

His mother sat down beside him. She smoothed the hair back from his forehead. "You know, we can't always have everything exactly the way we want it," she said.

"Yeah, Mom. I know. Thanks, Mom."

He decided to go up to his room for a while.

He took the fielder's mitt from the mirror brace on his dresser. He poured on a few drops of neat's-foot oil and worked it into the leather. He sat on the bed.

"I'll show them," he muttered, hammering the pocket of the mitt with his fist. "I'll show them. I'll earn that money.

"I'll mow lawns.

"I'll clean garages.

"Baby-sit.

"Run errands.

"Anything. But I'm going to get that tool chest. I'm going to GET it," he said, pounding the mitt.

He was only vaguely aware of the telephone ringing and of his father's voice.

After a time, there was a knock at Johnny's door.

"Someone wants to speak to you on the telephone," his mother said.

When Johnny put the receiver to his ear, he did not recognize the voice that spoke to him.

"Hello, Johnny," a man's voice said. "I've just been talking to your father. Great job you did on those animals, Johnny. Saw the picture in the paper this morning. Great idea, that was, posing your sister on that wooden buffalo. And, say, that was some buffalo."

Here the man was seized with laughing that went on for some time.

"Terrific," he managed to say at last. "Gave us quite an idea here at the fair grounds."

"Fair grounds?" Johnny repeated.

"That's right, Johnny. Now here's the thing. We're beginning to get things set up for the fair next month. Those big animals you

88

built and your sister sitting on that buffalo gave us an idea.

"Now here's what we want to do. We want to build a regular side-show for kids—a side-show with a lot of animals and things for kids to climb around on. We might start with those two you made for the contest if you'll sell them to us."

"Sure. Gee, that's—" Johnny said.

"But we want lots more," the man went on. "And, Johnny, we think you are just the one to give us the ideas for that kind of a side-show. We want you to show us how to build things kids will like. We'll pay you, of course. There's a lot to do before the fair opens. It's going to be work. Hard work. But you don't mind a little work, do you, Johnny?"

"Oh, no, sir. I don't mind," Johnny said. He thought about it for a few moments. "I don't mind. The fact is, I'm used to it."

"Good. Now, your father said he would be glad to bring you over to the fair grounds this afternoon. I asked him to come along so we can make sure everything is okay with everybody. Okay?"

"Oh, okay. I mean all right, Sir. Sure. Okay," Johnny said.

When he hung up the phone, Johnny drew a deep breath and then yelled,

"OH BOY!"

He grabbed Nancy and swung her around.

"Nancy, old kid, we're famous."

"I think it's just wonderful," Mrs. Thornton said.

# A Job

That afternoon on the way to the fair grounds Johnny said, "I've already got some ideas for building more animals and things. Really big ones. I think I'll do dinosaurs for a while."

Then he said, "You know, Nancy helped a lot with all this. She handles tools pretty well—for a girl, that is. I think I'll get her something real nice with some of the money I earn at the fair grounds. After I get the tool chest, I mean," he added hastily. "There ought to be enough money to do both, don't you think?"

Mr. Thornton laughed. "I think so," he said. He drove up to the fair ground gates.

"Yes, sir, you're expected," the guard said when Mr. Thornton told him their names. The gate swung open.

The car moved along the deserted midway. "I never saw it like this," Johnny said. "It looks strange without people."

"They'll be here when the fair opens," Mr. Thornton said.

When Johnny and Mr. Thornton were walking toward the steps of the administration building, Mr. Thornton said, "Remember, Son, the decisions will be yours. I'll just be sitting in as a sort of impartial judge. You can ask me anything you want to ask about the business arrangements between you and the fair ground officials. But I will leave the decisions to you."

"Thanks," Johnny said. "Thanks, Dad. And, by the way, I think I'll be able to pay for that tool chest all by myself."